Dear Parent:
Your child's love of reading starts here!

Every child learns to read in a different way and at his or her own speed.
You can help your young reader improve and become more confident
by encouraging his or her own interests and abilities. You can also guide
your child's spiritual development by reading stories with biblical values
and Bible stories, like I Can Read! books published by Zonderkidz. From
books your child reads with you to the first books he or she reads alone,
there are I Can Read! books for every stage of reading:

SHARED READING
Basic language, word repetition, and whimsical
illustrations, ideal for sharing with your emergent reader.

BEGINNING READING
Short sentences, familiar words, and simple concepts for
children eager to read on their own.

READING WITH HELP
Engaging stories, longer sentences, and language play
for developing readers.

READING ALONE
Complex plots, challenging vocabulary, and high-interest
topics for the independent reader.

ADVANCED READING
Short paragraphs, chapters, and exciting themes for the
perfect bridge to chapter books.

I Can Read! books have introduced children to the joy of reading since
1957. Featuring award-winning authors and illustrators and a fabulous
cast of beloved characters, I Can Read! books set the standard for
beginning readers.

A lifetime of discovery begins with the magical words **"I Can Read!"**

Visit www.icanread.com for information on enriching your child's reading experience.
Visit www.zonderkidz.com for more Zonderkidz I Can Read! titles.

Where can I go from your Spirit?
Where can I flee from your presence?
—*Psalm 139:7*

ZONDERKIDZ

Little David and His Best Friend
Text copyright © 2010 by Crystal Bowman
Illustrations copyright © 2010 by Frank Endersby

Requests for information should be addressed to:
Zonderkidz, *Grand Rapids, Michigan 49530*

Library of Congress Cataloging-in-Publication Data

Bowman, Crystal.
    Little David and his best friend / by Crystal Bowman ; illustrated by Frank Endersby.
        p. cm.
    ISBN 978-0-310-71710-2 (softcover)
    [1. Mice—Fiction. 2. Friendship—Fiction. 3. Jealousy—Fiction. 4. Christian life—Fiction.] I.
    Endersby, Frank, ill. II. Title.
    PZ7.B6834Li 2010
    [E]—dc22   2008008370

Editor: Mary Hassinger
Art direction: Jody Langley

Printed in China

10 11 12 13 14 15 /SCC/ 6 5 4 3 2 1

I Can Read!

Little David
and
His Best Friend

story by Crystal Bowman

pictures by Frank Endersby

Little David liked to sing.

He also liked to play his harp.

The king liked David's songs.

"Live in my house!" said the king.

So David went to live with the king.

The king had a son named Jon.

David and Jon played outside.

"Race me to the stump!" said Jon.

David and Jon ran.

They got to the stump

at the same time.

"You are my best friend,"

Jon told David.

"And you are my best friend,"

David said to Jon.

One day some rats came to town.

Everyone was afraid.

The king said to little David,

"You are brave.

Chase those bullies away!"

David asked God to help him.

Little David got a big spoon.

Jon found a can.

David beat the spoon on the can.

The rats were afraid of the noise.

They ran far away.

All the mice were so happy.

"We love little David!" they cried.

"He is the best mouse in the land!"

The king was very mad about this.

He stomped on the floor.

"I am the king!" he said.

"I am the best!"

"Make little David go away,"

the king said to Jon.

Jon started to cry.

"David is my friend," he said.

"Please don't send him away."

The king did not want Jon to be sad.

But the mice liked David

more than they liked the king.

So the king did not change his mind.

"Send him away!" said the king.

Jon talked to little David.

"The king is mad," he said.

"I'm afraid he might hurt you.

You must go away."

Jon gave David a big hug.

"I will miss you," he said.

"God will keep you safe."

"Good-bye, Jon," said David.

"I will miss you too."

Little David left the king's house.

He ran and ran and ran.

David had a friend named Sam.

Sam lived far away.

He hoped that Sam would help him.

David knocked on Sam's door.

"Hello, David," said Sam.

"I am happy to see you."

David was tired and hungry.

"Sit down, David," said Sam.

"Have some milk and cheese."

David told Sam all about the king.

"You may stay here," said Sam.

"God will keep you safe

until you can go back."

Little David missed Jon.

But he knew that God was with Jon.

God was with David too,

no matter where he went.